CHAPTER ONE

BROOKE

The house I have known since I was a child suddenly seems like a strange, unforgiving maze. Countless family portraits and holiday pictures fly past my peripheral vision, but none of the pleasant, smiling faces can help me know.

I can hear his footsteps behind me. He does not seem to be in a hurry, which only deepens the intense, burning fear rushing through my body.

"Leave me alone!" I yell. In my desperate flight, my hip bangs into the old, heavy dresser in the hallway that used to belong to grandma. A few of mother's gaudy figurines fall to the floor as the pain shoots up through my left side.

A calm voice responds, closer than I had hoped: "I'm sorry, Ms. West, I cannot do that."

I was not expecting an answer. My brain is working overtime to think of a way to reach the front door without being caught.

The kitchen. I can run into the garden from there, squeeze through the bushes, and hope that Mr. Weissmann next door is home.

I take a sharp right, past my old room. It offered me comfort and safety for years, but now it would just be a dead end. My bags are still standing next to the bed; I was going to unpack as soon as my parents left for the party, but I had not expected Jennifer to call and talk for hours. Or that a scary man would suddenly be chasing me through the house.

What does he want with me? The thought keeps repeating in my mind, and I hope that the right answer is 'ransom' if I do not manage to escape. Dad has money, lots of it, after all.

I can see the bright lights in the kitchen ahead. I must have put some distance between me and him now, enough for me to escape through the door. If he had been running, he might have caught me. I dash for the door to the garden.

It refuses to open.

"Fuck!" I push as hard as I can, I bang on the glass while I scream for help. It takes me a few moments before I notice the stack of large, heavy garden tiles pushed against the door. The contractor still had not finished the new patio, and now this man has used the tiles to block my only escape.

No wonder he did not bother to run.

"Ms. West," the voice sounds behind me.

I turn around and face the home invader. He was shrouded in shadow when I first saw him as he suddenly appeared in the living room, but as he steps into the kitchen's bright lights, conflicting emotions erupt inside my body.

LOVINGLY KIDNAPPED
©2022 J.D. Ackles
All rights reserved
Published: J.D. Ackles 2022
Cover by J.D. Ackles

CONTENT WARNING

This story is not suitable for readers under the age of 18 due to its graphic sexual content. The themes of this story include BDSM, bondage, and DDLG. All characters portrayed are over 18 years old.

LOVINGLY

HIS WILLING VICTIM 1

KIDNAPPED

First, there is fear. It is pure, intense, and frightening, impossible to ignore.

Secondly, there is surprise. The strong-jawed face is handsome, beautiful even. His steely gray eyes stare at me with calm determination as he commands the room with his presence. His black clothes and gloves seem to swallow the light, bringing even more focus to his sharp features.

"What the fuck do you want?" I manage to grab a sharp knife from the block nearby and point it at the man. I cannot keep the fear from sneaking through my trembling voice.

The man stops. "I want to take you, Ms. West."

"Like what, on a fucking date?" *Good job, Brooke. Sarcasm.*

The narrow lips open in a warm smile. "Not a date, unfortunately. Though you are a very beautiful woman." Confidence hangs around him like a dense cloud. He steps towards me, ignoring the knife in my hand. His black leather jacket squeaks as he moves, and the dark biker boots create a disturbing beat on the marble floor. "Your father owes money to a few unsavory types, and they have hired me and my associate to help collect what they're owed."

How is he staying this calm?

I clench the knife, but the man's cool demeanor is throwing me off. I have seen enough horror movies to know that it is bad to see the face of your kidnapper, yet this man does not attempt to hide his chiseled looks. My brain is trying to find a way out, yet somehow it keeps drawing my attention towards the fact that I risk being kidnapped in my panties and a Blink 182 tank top that is one size too small and showing my midriff.

"Can I convince you to lower that knife, Ms. West?" He reaches out a hand. "There is no need for this to be more unpleasant than absolutely necessary. I am a professional, after all."

"A professional *kidnapper?*" I cannot help but chuckle at the absurdity of the conversation I am having. "Who the fuck was your guidance counselor in high school?"

He lowers his arm and smirks. His shoulders relax, but a second later, he lunges towards me with a sudden burst of speed that I am unprepared for. The knife slices through his jacket, but it is not a deep cut; his strong hand closes around my wrist, squeezing it tight, forcing me to drop the blade. For a second, I am distracted by the smell of leather and the subtle hint of expensive cologne. He pulls my arm behind my back, yanking it upwards, while his other arm grabs me in a chokehold.

I struggle and kick, but he is too strong.

"Ms. West, I need you to be more cooperative." The feel of his muscular arm against my throat pacifies me instantly like a cat grabbed by the neck. He tightens his grip. "I assure you, I have no interest in hurting you." A drop of blood falls from his arm onto the floor. "Nod if you understand."

The rational, analytical part of my brain, the one that is crushing it in Thermodynamics this semester, tries to fight through the haze of fear and anxiety. I know that there is no point in trying to fight this man. He is in complete control and has seemingly done this countless times before. I can feel the heat of his body through the leather jacket, his calm breath on my ear. No amount of morning runs and yoga classes can help this five-foot-seven student take down a beast like him.

If I resist, he might injure me, lessening my chance of escape at a later point.

I nod. The irrational, rebellious brat inside sighs in frustration.

"Very good," he says and removes his arm from my neck, but he still has a firm grip on my arm. "I do need to tie you up, I hope you understand."

I feel narrow, cold steel against my skin as he handcuffs the wrist he is holding. I have never been restrained before, and the unwelcome sensation fills me with dread. He tightens the cuffs, and I let out a surprised, frightened gasp.

"The other hand, if you would be so kind." I can hear the smile in his voice. There is a subtle threat looming behind his unnaturally soft words, and I slowly move my other arm as if it was an involuntary reflex.

"Thank you."

"You're welcome." The words stumble past my quivering lips, surprising us both. *What the fuck?*

I hear a muted chuckle behind me as he handcuffs the other wrist. "There, I hope they're not too uncomfortable."

He finds a roll of duct tape in his jacket pocket and squats to tie my ankles. My body shivers as his hands graze my calves, and I wonder if he is hoping to get a glorified review online after the whole ordeal. '5 stars, would let him kidnap me again.' The fear still has its cold hands firmly closed around my throat, but I am not panicking as much as I probably should. What is it about this man's aura that is soothing my instinct to fight or run?

He adds another few rounds of tape around my thighs. I struggle to stand upright, but he steadies my body. The characteristic sound of tape being torn sounds one more time as he looks at me with a smile. Somehow, the idea of being gagged scares me more than being tied up.

"I … I promise I won't scream."

He shakes his head. "You'll forgive me if I don't tend to put a lot of trust in the promises of kidnapping victims, Miss."

I cannot help but stare into his deep, dark pupils that threaten to swallow me as he tapes my lips shut. A few more strips of tape are added to ensure that nothing but a pleading moan escapes me. Jennifer always told me that I need to try bondage, but this was likely not what she had in mind. Or maybe it was, she can be a bit weird at times.

He takes a step back as if he needs to admire his creation, his masterpiece. He scratches the impeccably kept stubble on his chin and nods approvingly. I do not know if it is directed at me or his taping skills. "I'm going to lie you down on the floor for a bit, Miss. Your antics earlier have caused me to spill DNA onto your father's expensive floor."

His strong arms grab me and lie me down. The marble feels cold against my bare stomach and legs. I look up at my kidnapper as he removes his jacket and wipes the blood from his arm with a paper towel, carefully depositing the red sheets into his pocket. He places a clean cloth from a nearby rack onto his arm and uses the duct tape to create a makeshift bandage. Toned muscles are visible beneath the dark blue T-shirt, and a few stylish tattoos peek out from under the sleeve. His face is set in stone as he meticulously cleans any surface that he has bled on.

A professional, indeed.

CHAPTER TWO

CONNOR

I have to focus. Concentrate. This is just another job, another business transaction. They hire me because I am good at what I do, maybe even the best. For a second, I catch myself being annoyed at the hole in my favorite jacket. It was expensive.

Focus on the job, Connor. I push the frustration aside. I had not expected the petite girl to fight back, and I wonder if my concentration wavered for a second as I attacked her, allowing her to draw blood. I glance at her writhing body on the marble floor, hoping she will not notice. The handcuffs clatter against the hard surface as she tests her restraints, but she will not escape. I have done this too many times, though my victims are not usually this young.

Or this hot.

The blue tank top does little to hide the enticing body beneath, including her breasts. The cold floor has made her nipples erect, and I cannot help but feel my dick harden at the sight. She catches me staring; there is fear in the expressive hazel eyes, but stubbornness too. A frustrated groan escapes the gag. She is young, probably in her early twenties, at least ten years my junior. The world has not been cruel to her, and her pristine face does not look like it has faced much hardship. The long, black hair flows onto the floor like a river and looks like something out of a shampoo commercial.

Her shampoo probably costs more than my first car did. Rich people. I do derive a certain pleasure from throwing a wrench in their perfect lives.

I inspect the kitchen one last time, but I find no signs of my blood anywhere. The wound stings, but the cut is superficial, harmless. Just like she seemed at first glance. There is something about her resilience, her sheer fucking *balls* that intrigues me. She attacked a former Special Forces marine with a knife and managed to wound him. She did not beg when I grabbed her. She did not cry.

At least not yet. Crow might change that. I shudder at the thought.

"I think I'm just about ready to go," I say and put my jacket back on. I have already spent too long in here, but there is no need to panic or be impolite. This girl has done me no real harm, and we do not get paid any faster for scaring the victim. "Let me escort you out of here." Her eyes widen as I pull a black cloth bag from my pocket and put it over her head.

She is lighter than I thought. No need to call for Crow to assist. She whimpers as I sling her over my shoulder and walk towards the exit, being careful not to bump her head on the door frames or any of the overpriced knick-knacks pestering the hallways. My hands have a firm grip on her strong thighs, and I can feel her abs tense up against my shoulder. A warm, pleasant sensation ripples through my body as the scent of lilacs reach my nose.

Don't get distracted. She is just another job.

Crow gets out of the black BMW and opens the trunk of the sedan the moment I step outside. The moonlight falls on his unappealing, scarred face, and the wry smile only serves to make him look even more like the villain he is.

"Thank God for rich people and their need for privacy," he says and nods towards the dense, tall hedge shielding us from curious neighbors. The West family estate sits comfortably in the middle of the city's richest community. It is not the first time Crow and I have picked up a prize in this part of town, but people rarely make a fuss when their loved ones are kidnapped. They usually have the money to sort it all out, after all, and none of them wants to reveal what type of people, they have been dealing with.

Even though half of them have dealings with the Irish. I snicker to myself as I gently place Brooke West in the trunk of the car.

Crow looks at the squirming girl and licks his lips. "That is a nice body." His gravelly voice is dripping with lust and menace. "I might need to have a go with her later."

Brooke shakes her head violently while protesting through her gag.

"That is not how we do it," I say and slam the trunk shut.

The car ride is silent, as it should be. Crow does not say a word, but I can hear his teeth grinding. He has stepped out of line before, occasionally roughing up a victim more than was needed, but I have to assume that he can keep his temper under control. And his dick in his pants. No sound can be heard from the trunk, no muffled cries for help or desperate struggling.

Brooke is quiet and still as I pull her from the trunk. It usually means that the victim is paralyzed with fear, maybe even resigned to their fate, but this is no ordinary victim. She is not as vapid as most of the people that run afoul of the Irish. She is biding her time, analyzing the situation, listening.

"Don't try anything, Ms. West. It's for your own good," I whisper, low enough that Crow, who has gone ahead to prepare the room, cannot hear me.

No response.

The abandoned factory is one of several locations made available to us by our benevolent employers. It reeks of mold, and the old machines are glazed in a thick layer of grime and dust. Many tears have been soaked up by these concrete floors, both before and after Crow and I started using the eerie halls for our nefarious purposes a few years ago.

I sit her down on the chair in the middle of the old storage room. It is a thoroughly depressing place. The naked concrete walls, the lack of windows, the thick steel door – any semblance of optimism and happiness is quickly drowned in here, and I already long to finish the job, collect my sizeable paycheck and leave for my luxurious apartment in the Caribbean until they call for me again. I place her delicate, cuffed hands behind the backrest before cutting her feet and thighs loose from the duct tape, only to tape her ankles to the chair legs. I grab the short chain hanging lazily from the chair and connect it to the handcuffs with a padlock, ensuring that she has no way of escape.

Every scenario is accounted for; years of experience, including a few desperate chases when someone managed to escape, has led me to this point. I know what I am doing. I am in control of the situation.

Then what is that unsettling sensation in my stomach? It is foreign to me, and it manages to get more intense when I remove the black hood from Brooke. She blinks a few times, tests her restraints, but there is no trace of panic on her flawless face.

"I am going to have a look around, make sure no homeless idiots have found the hole in the fence," Crow says. His dark eyes linger on Brooke, but she makes sure not to meet his lustful gaze. "You stay with the broad."

I nod. He slams the heavy door behind him.

The flickering, naked lightbulb struggles to illuminate the small room, but it does not detract from her beauty. Her pupils are fully dilated as they look up at me with a defiant stare. I grab the burner phone in my pocket and take a picture of her. Her eyes widen in surprise before a skeptical wrinkle appears between her dark eyebrows.

"For your father. An incentive." I send the picture to the number I have been given. They will take it from here. I am not part of the negotiation, I just procure the object of desire. "I am going to remove your gag now. Your first instinct will be to scream for help, but I assure you, it won't do you any good here. And the acoustics in here are terrible."

"Auch!" she groans as I tear the layers of tape from her mouth. "You really know how to show a lady a good time."

I smile at her moxie. "I do, actually. I have never had any complaints."

"You might get a few from me." She moves in the chair, tests her restraints again. "Is this necessary? I promise I will be a good girl." She pouts as she looks up at me.

"That won't get you anywhere, Ms. West."

The pout turns into a white, disarming smile. "Please, call me Brooke."

"No." I take the water bottle from the small table in the corner and put a straw in it. "Here. Drink something. It could be a long night."

I can tell that her first instinct is to refuse it, to defy me, but the rational part of her brain wins the argument. She knows she will need her strength if she wants any hope of escaping. Her sarcasm and the delightful smile have no effect, and it looks like she has realized that by now as her face finds a more brooding expression befitting the situation.

"I am sorry that an innocent woman like yourself has ended up in a situation like this." I pull another chair over and sit down in front of her. "I promise you it is strictly business."

She rolls her eyes. "Don't try to downplay this. You fucking *kidnapped* me!"

I shrug. "Yeah, so? Would you prefer my employers simply shot your father? If everything goes smoothly, your stay here will be short, and you'll be back to fucking frat boys with your Phi Bitch Beta sorority sisters as soon as the holidays are over." I cough, trying to calm my temper. I hate spoiled, entitled girls.

"I still don't get what my dad has to do with all this." She leans forward as far as her restraints will let her. The long hair frames her face as if it was a Da Vinci painting, a vision of beauty. "He is a lawyer. A boring one."

"Who has dealings with the Irish Mafia, my bosses." I take off my leather jacket and roll up the sleeve on my T-shirt, showing her the three-leaf clover tattoo. "See? They are not to be messed with. He made a few bad deals on their behalf, and now they want their money back. He probably only needs to liquidate a few assets to ensure your release."

Her eyes flicker for a second as if she is trying to process the information. "I … my father …" She pauses and leans back in the chair. "You keep saying 'they', not 'we'. Why?"

Getting to know your captor, build a rapport. Smart. It won't work, sweetie.

"You can call me an 'independent contractor'. I have no direct ties to the mafia anymore, too messy." *Why am I telling her this?*

She nods at the door. "And your associate strives for the same professionalism?"

Ouch. "Of course," I lie.

She does not believe me. Why would she? I can tell that the questions are burning her tongue, that the fear is hiding just beneath the surface. She is trying to retain control as much as I am.

"I …" She clenches her jaw, and the fear peeks through the façade for a short moment. "Why no masks, then? It can't be good for business." She tries to look me in the eye but fails.

I try to defuse the tension with a chuckle. "We know how to stay hidden. Besides, no one wants to admit that they have had dealings with the mob. I met a former kidnapping victim at a garden party not long ago, he nodded politely and made sure to stay at the other end of the garden the whole time." I check my watch. "I need to go update my employer. I will be back soon. You stay here."

She groans at the bad joke. "Fuck you."

CHAPTER THREE

BROOKE

It is cold in the small room. I try to suppress the panic that threatens to take hold as he closes and locks the steel door behind him. All my energy has been spent putting on a brave face, and I can feel the fear rise as the unnerving silence envelops me. I want to hate my kidnapper, the pleasant, business-like man with the face of a rugged angel, but somehow, all my anger and frustration causing the vein in my neck to pulsate is aimed towards my father. The idiot. I should be surprised that he has been dealing with the mafia, but I am not. He was always a sucker for a quick profit, and it is only blind luck that has ensured our family's fortune.

"Fat load of good that money does me now," I mumble to myself. My cheeks still burn from when Mr. Handsome tore the duct tape off, and my wrists ache from the tight handcuffs. I test my restraints one more time. Maybe an elf picked the lock since I tried last time.

No such luck.

Try to calm down. You're worth nothing to them if you're dead.

The kidnapper's calm, gray eyes keep appearing in my mind. Why can I not stop thinking about him? The image of his cocky smile, the annoyingly perfect thick, dark hair, the feel of his strong muscles under the leather jacket as he carried me, all should be filling me with disgust. But it is not.

The door opens, but it is not him. It is his scary associate.

"All alone, I see?" The scarred face opens in a yellow, unsettling smile. He stinks of cigarettes, and his thin hair is combed back with way too much product. The smile reminds me of a comic book supervillain. *This* is how a kidnapper looks. Terrifying. Unpredictable.

Horny? *Fuck.*

He closes the door and removes his black bomber jacket. He is no less ripped than the other kidnapper, but the tattoos are far more disturbing. I know enough latin to recognize that most of the quotes refer to death.

"They call me Crow," he says, bringing his face close to mine. His breath makes me gag.

"I didn't ask." My lower lip is quivering, undermining my pitiful attempt at defiance. I am all too aware that I am helpless to do anything.

The smile seems permanently etched into his face. I know what he wants. I know he is going to get it. I know I can likely dissuade him, as I have done with men in the past, but they were drunk or high. This man is a psychopath; I can see it in his eyes. It is the same self-assured, invincible look I have seen in so many of the successful men my father has brought home for dinner over the years. No empathy. No compassion.

His gloved hand grabs my breast. I feel like I could throw up at any moment. "Firm. I like that." He lifts my shirt over my breasts and tucks in the fabric to ensure that it stays there. He continues to feel me up with the grace of a bulldozer. One hand starts moving down my torso, across my stomach, towards my panties. I clench my jaw in anticipation as every fiber in my body begs me to act.

"Don't …" It sounds like I am begging, but in my mind, it is a warning.

He laughs. It is the most unpleasant, spiteful laugh I have ever heard. "What are you going to do, little lady? I know your type." He still has one hand on my breast. The other is moving up my inner thigh. "You try to act all confident and independent, but in the end, you just want a strong man to take control."

His face is very close now.

Too close.

"AAAARGH, FUCK!"

My forehead hits him in the nose, sending blood spurting onto the floor and my face. I cannot help but grin, even though I know that this is going to cost me. His payback is swift and fierce. My cheek explodes in pain as his fist makes contact.

"Do you like that, you bitch?" he shouts, his voice breaking.

I can taste blood. "Go fuck yourself, you bastard!"

A second punch lands in the same place while I am still screaming. I almost fall over from the force of the impact.

He is going to kill me. My mind is fighting my body, both trying to figure out the best way to handle the situation as he raises his hand to continue the beating.

The door bursts open. The other man lunges towards Crow and pulls him away, throwing him against the wall. The calm, cool exterior that had defined the handsome kidnapper up until now is cracking at the seams; throbbing veins are visible on his temples like rivers of fury, and he clenches his fist so hard that the muscles in his upper arm threaten to tear the T-shirt.

"Get the *fuck* out, Crow!" He points at the bloodied man, his teeth bared like a predator, his voice dripping with determination. "This is not how we handle things! Touch her again and I will *end* you!"

Crow seems to shrink as he is faced with the barely contained wrath of his associate. "She fucking headbutted me, Connor!"

"I don't care!" The man takes a step forward, causing Crow to squirm. "I can handle this myself, get out of here!"

"You can't just tell me to …"

"You'll still get paid." Connor lowers his accusing finger, but his other hand is still clenched in a tight fist. "Go find a cheap whore somewhere to pass the time."

Crow glares at me with hateful eyes, trying to calm himself. "Fine. You deal with this cunt. She isn't worth it, anyway. But if you blow this …"

"I won't."

The two men stare at each other for what feels like an eternity. My jaw is on fire from the rough treatment, but I cannot take my eyes away from the towering beast of a man standing between me and Crow. When Crow finally nods and leaves with a sulk, I realize that I have been holding my breath and gasps.

Connor turns around and looks at me as if he only now notices my presence. The fire in his eyes seems to fade, replaced by a concerned frown.

"I'll be right back," he says, leaving the room for a bit before returning with an ice pack. He kneels in front of my chair and gently presses the pack against my bruised chin. "I'm sorry about that." The is a hint of genuine concern in his voice, but it is still firm and professional. "You handled yourself well."

I wince in pain. "It is not the first time I've broken the nose of a guy that came too close."

"Is that so?" He smiles. "I guess I shouldn't be surprised that Crow isn't the first man to make an inappropriate pass at you."

"He isn't, but I'm usually not tied to a chair when a man tries to get with me." I demonstratively rattle the chains connecting my handcuffs.

"I am going to keep you like this for now, even if it is uncomfortable."

For some reason, I am okay with that.

"In any case, you better not try that stunt with me, Ms. West."

It feels like I am being scolded by the teacher after being caught smoking during recess. I have no idea why I am enjoying it. Connor rests a hand on my shoulder as he holds the ice pack to my face, and a pleasant shiver runs down my spine from his touch.

"Are you also going to punch a helpless girl if I misbehave?" I say and bite my lip. *Am I flirting with this guy? He KIDNAPPED me!* The boring, rational voice berates me, but the intensity of the situation only makes it all … hotter.

He looks at me with a raised eyebrow. "I would not punch you, though I would hardly call you 'helpless'." A discreet crease appears at the corner of his mouth. "But I could find other ways to punish a little girl that doesn't know her place."

His deep, commanding voice causes every word to light a fire in my loins. He stands up, crosses his arms, and lets his eyes inspect every part of my body. He is older than me, older than any man I have been with. Well, I say 'man', but they have all been boys. Cocky jocks and a few sensitive poets, but all of them were far too insecure when the door to the bedroom closed. Connor is nothing like them. I have no doubt in my mind that I would still be sitting on this chair with my hands politely folded in my lap if I was not tied up, simply because he had told me to stay.

"I can't promise that I will behave," I say and move my thighs over the edge of the seat, spreading my legs. The voice telling me that this is wrong is now distant background music.

"Then I will make you." He removes his gloves.

I believe him. I want him to. I want *him*. He leans in over me, eclipsing the lightbulb above. I cannot see his face, but I feel his warm breath, the stubble on his chin the moment before his lips meet mine. It is a strong kiss, forceful even, but I do not resist as his tongue slips inside my mouth. His hand appears behind my neck, pushing our faces even closer together. The intensity overwhelms me, makes me realize that I have been kissed hundreds of times but never truly *kissed* anyone. I should protest, I should go two-for-two on broken noses, but every ounce of defiance melts away in the intoxicating cocktail of scratchy stubble, soft lifts, and insistent tongue.

Damn, you're in trouble now, Brooke.

"Did you enjoy that, Darling?" he asks me. 'Darling'. I should laugh, ask him if he thinks heaven is missing an angel, but somehow, it fits. From his mouth, any trashy pickup line that would have caused me to throw a drink in any other guy's face becomes a magic spell. "I asked you a question, Darling."

"I did, Conn…" His name sounds insufficient, even though I like it.

His hand is still on my neck as he pulls back slightly, allowing the light to illuminate his face. He smiles. "Call me 'Sir'. Or 'Daddy'. Whichever you prefer."

"I liked it, Daddy." The word rolls off my tongue, cementing the connection. It sounds right, beautiful. A few moments ago, I would have scoffed at any woman that could get herself to call a man 'daddy', but I get it now. The words seem to ignite something in Connor; I can see it in his eyes, those deep, hypnotizing eyes. My body is drawing him in, my legs are spread, welcoming him. He tries to retain control, but we both know he will have to give in.

"Are you trying to tempt me, Darling?" he asks, rubbing his lower lip with his thumb.

"Maybe I am. Do you like what you see?"

He nods. "I do."

Connor gets up and circles me a few times, letting his fingers graze my hair and shoulders, teasing me. Every soft touch sends a jolt of lust through me, and I can feel my panties getting wet. I squirm against my restraints, pull at the handcuffs – I want to touch him, but I am being denied, and it only adds to the pleasure. He stops behind me. Two strong hands touch my shoulders. His fingertips are soft, but there are callouses on his palms, and even with his feather-like touch, I can barely contain myself.

"You are not going to give me any trouble, are you, Darling?" His stubble touches the upper part of my ear as he whispers. His words cause my pussy to ache even more.

I want to be bratty, to try and wrestle some of the control away from him, but I do not want him to stop touching me. "No, Daddy."

His hands start their journey downward. My breasts are still exposed after Crow's ill-fated attempt, and Connor takes advantage of it. I cannot contain the moan that escapes me as he touches them. He has an artist's touch, treating them like priceless artifacts, not a stubborn dough that requires kneading. I do not mind passionate, rough breast play, but at this moment, his slow, meticulous touch is exactly what I need.

"That feels so good, Daddy ..." I whimper, biting my lip as he starts teasing my nipples. "I want mo… AUCH!"

He playfully pinches my nipple, catching me by surprise. "You do not get to demand anything of me, Darling. You may ask, but you are not in control. Do you understand?"

God, this is so hot. "Yes, Daddy. Sorry, Daddy."

CHAPTER FOUR

CONNOR

Strands of her hair caress my face as my hands move further down. She smells amazing, intoxicating. Muted gasps and pleased moans dance on her full, red lips. I look down and see her opening and closing her hands, embracing every touch of my fingers. The worn handcuffs, used on many unwilling victims, have left marks on her tanned skin, but I can tell that they add to her enjoyment, the way she keeps touching them to remind herself of her predicament.

I am in control. She is my little girl do with as I please, but I have a hard time ignoring the voice in the back of my head, itching like a mosquito bite in my brain, that is telling me that there is something deeper at work here. I want to possess her, to keep her, and yet I yearn for every word of desire and affection from her lips.

She shivers as I move my hand over her belly; she is ticklish there. I make note of it before I allow my fingers to trace the edge of her black panties. My cock hardens as a loud gasp escapes her and those pearly white, perfect teeth bite her lower lip. She is not used to relinquishing control. Even though she is helpless, she wants to direct me, to ask for more.

"Are you wet for me under here?" I ask, whispering in her ear.

"Mhmm …" Her eyes are closed. She is taking it all in. The chain connecting her wrists rattle as she tries to move closer to my hand. She groans as I pull it away.

I move in front of her and kneel. "Are you scared of me, Darling?"

She looks at me and seems to ponder the question for a moment. She should be, and she knows it. But there is untamed lust in those expressive eyes. She shakes her head. "No, Daddy. I am not."

Brooke flinches as I pull out my switchblade and flicks it open. The sharpened steel glows in the yellow light. I let it run up her inner thigh; her breathing is rapid, her body frozen, but I know at that moment that I could never hurt her. Not for real. With two precise cuts, I remove her panties and put the knife away.

"Do you want me to pleasure you, little Darling?" I let my fingers walk slowly up her thigh. I can feel the goosebumps on her skin. Is it the cold? No. Her cheeks are blushing, her eyes wide with anticipation.

"Yes, please, Daddy." Once more, she tries to move her lower body closer to my hand, and she sighs in frustration when she fails again.

It makes me so fucking horny when she calls me Daddy. I finally allow one finger to travel across her welcoming, pink slit. She is soaking wet, and it only serves to make me harder. She whimpers when I do not follow up right away. Her pussy is a gazelle, my fingers are a pack of lions stalking their prey, teasing it.

"Fuck …" she says as a breath catches in her throat.

I slap her breast. Not too hard, but enough to elicit a response; she cries out in surprise, but the hit arouses her. She sucks her lips in between her teeth and arches her back.

"Language, little Darling," I say in a stern voice that is not quite my own. "Unruly brats don't get rewarded."

She smiles. It is a devious, playful smile, one that makes the hairs on my neck stand up and a pleasant shiver run down my spine and nestle in my hard cock. "I'm sorry, Daddy. I promise I will be a good girl." She opens her legs even wider and sends me a sultry look. The bruise on her cheek only makes her look even more like a naughty girl looking for trouble.

Fuck, who is this girl?

I get up and lean in over her, once again grabbing her by her long, soft hair. I pull her in for a kiss. It is more for my benefit; I want to feel those amazing lips on mine again. Her mouth opens, inviting me in, but I keep my tongue in its home. Instead, hers comes to visit, and the moment it does, I slip my finger inside her wet, warm pussy. Her entire body quivers from my touch as I explore her, slowly, carefully, gently. I pull her hair, forcing her head away from my lips. Her mouth stays open, moaning as I kiss her exposed neck.

Another finger joins in. I move my head down, using my mouth to create a vacuum around her nipple, sucking it into my mouth. The moaning increases and her breathing is heavier now. I feel powerful and godlike, in control of this woman's pleasure. It does not matter that she is restrained at this moment, but it turns me on that she is.

"Please … Please, Daddy, rub my clit, won't you?"

I oblige. She asked nicely, after all. The two fingers inside her continue to search for spots of pure pleasure while my thumb starts circling her clit. Once more, her back arches as she yearns for more. I am all but certain that she has forgotten about her predicament at this moment, all that matters is the lust, the lust that we both share. I am tempted to give in to it, to untie her and fuck her, but it would not be proper.

Not yet.

But it is hard for me to withstand the temptation. Her pussy is tight around my fingers, and it is causing my cock to strain against the rough fabric of my black jeans. I want to be inside her, to feel that warm, soft pussy envelop me. I spread my fingers, sliding them up and down the walls. Her thighs are shaking from barely contained desire, and her abs tighten, visible through the flawless, tanned skin of her stomach.

I want her to come. To scream my name. But not yet.

"No! Daddy, please!" she cries when I stop rubbing her clit. Her eyes are manic as they look down at my grinning face. "I will do anything! Please let me come!" The voice of the confident college student has been replaced by the pleading whimper of a pitiful brat, and I am loving it.

"Will you be a good little girl if I do, Darling?"

She nods furiously. "Yes! Yes, I will! Please!"

I let go of her hair and bury my face between her legs. I slip a third finger inside her, stretching the soaking pussy, as a long, wet stroke of my tongue slides across her clit. The entire chair shakes as I apply more and more pressure with my skilled tongue, and though I cannot see her face, I know it is smiling.

Fuck, even her pussy smells good. The short pubic hair tickles my nose as I suck her clit inside my mouth to increase her pleasure.

"Daddy, I am so close! Can I come?" The words are barely intelligible, mixed in with moans and whines.

She is learning fast, already asking permission. I let her stew for a bit before answering, and I can see those enticing abs appear even clearer on her stomach. She is trying to stem the tide. "You may come," I say, briefly letting go of her clit. "Scream my name, Darling."

"Thank you, Daddyyyy ..." The words turn into a prolonged, primal scream. The chair creaks under the strain as the muscles in her arms and legs fight their bonds and her entire body tries to pull away. I do not stop licking, nor do my fingers stop their relentless pummeling of her pussy, not until her body twitches in response, signaling that the rolling thunder of the mighty orgasm has faded.

A curious silence settles in the small room, but the air is thick with sexual tension and lust. She is trying to catch her breath, and she closes her legs the moment I stand up. I am gripped by a sudden burst of modesty and roll down her tank top to cover her breasts, though her pussy still tempts me.

"That ... that was not unpleasant," she says. A warm, charming smile has nestled on the red-cheeked face. Darling is gone, for now, but the beautiful woman before me is no less hot than the submissive brat I just licked to orgasm.

I allow her to drink again, but this time our eyes are locked as she swallows the cold drink.

"You are still my captive, Brooke." I sit down on the chair across from her, doing my best to hide the rock-hard erection still filling my pants. "I … I am not going to set you free." Part of me wants to, but two things are stopping me; first of all, I do not want to wash up in a few days as a bloated corpse on the shoreline, but most of all, I do not want to risk losing her.

"I know." She moves in the chair as if she only now realizes how uncomfortable she is. "I wish you would, though." She smiles and nods at my crotch. "I could return the favor."

Is she playing with me? Is she just trying to find a way to escape? Do I care?

I chuckle. "I might let you." I want her to do it. Right now. My cock is protesting, pushing against my pants, begging to be let out.

"How does one end up in this line of business?" she asks and cocks her head. The black hair cascades onto her shoulder.

I lean back in the chair, wondering how much to reveal. "Considering the environment I grew up in, the people I knew, this was the … less messy choice." I both want to fuck this woman and hug her. What the hell is wrong with me? "I am sorry you got caught up in this."

She sighs. "Yeah … my fucking dad …"

"We don't choose our parents." The words scratch at old wounds and never offered me any comfort in the past, but they seem appropriate.

That cursed smile. It lights up her face and makes her look like a goddess, reels me in. "No, we don't."

I check the time; I have a set schedule to follow, and I have no idea how she will look at me after the next part. I am about to get up when her smile turns crooked and Darling returns.

"About that blowjob ... Daddy." She leans forward as far as her handcuffs will allow. "I am good at it. I have sucked many cocks."

I start sweating. "That does not seem appropriate for a little, innocent girl, Darling."

"I never claimed to be innocent." The tip of her tongue dances across her upper lip.

But you are. You haven't seen anything, my dear.

I stand up. My cock is leaving me no choice, and the rational part of my brain has started trying to justify it as well. She looks up at me and purses her lips. I should tell her not to try anything, but I know it is not necessary. Besides, the door is locked, she is handcuffed, pantyless, and there is a tall fence circling the property. I cut the duct tape holding her ankles with my knife. She responds by slowly and seductively crossing her legs.

The padlock is removed. She moves her arms over the armrest and sits on the edge of the chair, looking at me with a disappointed pout. "Are you going to keep my hands cuffed behind my back? Would you expect Picasso to paint without arms?"

"Are you being difficult, Darling?" I cross my arms and scowl.

She looks at the ground. "No, Daddy. I ... I just want to please you, that is all."

Oh, she's good.

"Then I will do you this one favor, little Darling. And you will repay me."

She nods. I unlock one hand from the cuffs and immediately lock it back on after pulling her hands to the front. Brooke looks at the cuffs for a few seconds, letting her fingers run across the scratched steel.

"I think I like being handcuffed," she says, seemingly as surprised to hear the words coming out of her mouth as I am. She smiles as she rattles the chain. "Is this the kind of jewelry I can expect from you, Daddy?"

"As long as it looks this good on you, yes." I pause to ponder the implications of our exchange. Are we still flirting, or is she feeling a deeper connection? Am I? The thought is pushed away the moment she unbuckles my belt and opens the zipper.

"Oh, Daddy … you're *huge!*" she says with her most bratty, almost childish, voice as she pulls my cock out. She licks her lips as she winks at me. "May I?"

I nod. I crave her mouth on me, but I do not show it. She may be the one in handcuffs, but I feel trapped as her soft hand gently strokes the shaft; her touch is light as a feather, teasing me. She cocks her head as if she is studying it, mapping uncharted territory. *If I have my way, you will become very familiar with it, my Darling.*

It is playful at first. Arousing. But it is not what I want. It is my turn.

I grab her long hair and force her to look up. "Are you toying with me, Darling?"

She smiles. "Maybe."

I shake my finger from side to side. "That is not a nice thing to do, little one. I want you to suck my cock. Suck it well. Are you going to do what I tell you?"

The full lips squeeze together in a pout. "Yes, Daddy." She tries to look insulted, but I know she wants it. I can see it in her eyes.

I guide her head forward, pressing my tip against her lips. She does not open up for me, not at first. She groans as I pull her hair and send her a stern look. With a bratty eye roll, she opens her mouth, allowing me inside. The silky smooth lips are divine on the sensitive skin, and any doubts I might have about her willingness are silenced a moment later when she pushes herself forward until the tip hits the back of her throat. Her tongue flattens against the underside, applying pressure.

"Shit, girl, that feels amazing!" I start fucking her mouth. She gags on my cock, but there are no protests, only pleased moans that join mine in a delightful choir, echoing between the hard, naked walls. The sharp metal edges of her handcuffs start scraping against my inner thigh as she fondles my balls and taint.

It is good. Amazing. *Too* amazing. I can feel the control slip out of my hands as her mouth does its dance up and down my saliva-drenched cock. At this moment, I am hers, her property. I will do anything to have her keep going, to keep her lips on me.

She knows it. Her mouth lets go; a string of drool connects her to me as she looks up and smiles. Her hands start sliding up and down the cock, painfully slow. "Do you like this, Daddy?"

"I do, Darling." I cannot keep the lust from adding a slight vibrato to my voice. "You better continue."

She cocks her head. "And what if I don't feel like it?"

"Don't challenge me." My voice hardens.

"What are you going to do, Daddy?"

I look down at her with a wry smile as I slide my black leather belt out of the belt loops. A tinge of fear enters her eyes, but I am not going to hit her.

Not yet, at least.

The fear turns to lust as I tie the belt around her neck and pull it, choking her slightly.

"Suck my cock, Darling." I pull her closer, and her stubbornness vanishes, turning into aroused submission.

She is loving this as much as I am.

It does not take long before a powerful orgasm shakes my body. My legs can barely keep me upright as I pull the belt, holding her fast as I fill her mouth. Her hands stroke the shaft as she swallows it. All of it.

"Thank you, Daddy," she says while she licks the last drops from the tip. The brat is subdued; the belt around her neck has served its purpose, reminding her who is in charge.

The fact that I have kidnapped her has nothing to do with it at this moment.

CHAPTER FIVE

BROOKE

No man has ever looked at me this way. No man has ever made me *come* before. I can still taste Connor's seed in my mouth as I meet his gaze, staring into those deep, complex eyes. I have never swallowed for anyone before, yet there was no question, no doubt in my mind as he filled my mouth. I want to please him, to be his, and yet I cannot stop myself from resisting when he gets possessive. It is a game we play, despite the serious circumstances. I am his captive. Every movement of my arms and hands reminds me of this as the handcuffs restrict me, yet I feel safe. Has he hypnotized me? Am I experiencing the fastest case of Stockholm Syndrome ever?

I cannot explain it, and I do not want to. Part of me knows that this cannot end well, but it only adds to the intensity.

It does not detract from the experience that the largest cock I have ever seen is hanging in front of me, visible out of the corner of my eye. *I am not done with you,* I think as I still look Connor in the eye, waiting for him to make the next move. Any move. My pussy is still tingling from the orgasm, and I want more. I want him inside me, yet it is not for me to decide.

"You are incredible, Brooke," he says, his breath still reeling from his orgasm. He smiles at me, but there is a sinister edge to it that both entices and scares me.

I remove a loose strand of hair from my eye. "Thanks." I lock the brat up in her cage for now. I can feel her close as if she is a new friend I have only just met but already know will be a close companion from now on. I sit back in the chair and cross my legs. "Do you do this with all the girls you kidnap?"

"Of course not." He pulls up his pants before he leans in and places a warm, passionate kiss on my lips.

A wave of relief washes over me. The kiss helps subdue the voice in the back of my mind that tries to tell me that he is using me, that he does not feel the same way I do. But even so, I cannot help but become acutely aware of my predicament as I once again see that sinister smile on his face.

"Tell me." I push him back. "What are you hiding?"

"Many things," he says and shrugs.

I shake my head. "That is not what I mean. The way you're looking at me – there's something you have to do, but you cannot figure out how I'm going to respond."

His eyes flicker for a moment. "How did you ...?" He smiles. "You're pretty good at reading people."

"Always have been. I know how I come across to most people, but I'm not stupid."

"I never said you were."

"So tell me."

Connor sighs and leans against the table. "My employer expects a video. Soon. A follow-up to the picture I took earlier, something to further motivate your father." He rubs the back of his neck, and I can tell that the professional is struggling with the situation. "We usually whip or beat the captive."

My hand involuntarily reaches for the bruise on my cheek. "I … Seriously?" Connor's presence can no longer keep the room's oppressive atmosphere at bay, and I feel like I cannot breathe.

Connor looks at me with a furrowed brow before the smile reappears. "It is not up for discussion. You do deserve punishment for toying with me before."

Something shifts inside me. My hand leaves the bruise and slides towards my neck where his belt still hangs. The feel of the leather against my skin, the leather that ignited a submissive spark I never knew existed, sends a warm glow through my body. "I'm sorry if I disappointed you, Daddy …"

He kneels in front of me. In a flash, his face becomes serious. Daddy is gone, so is the professional kidnapper. This is the Connor that I saw in flashes as he pleasured me. "Brooke, you need to be convincing." His deep voice is filled with concern and affection. "It's not just your dad that will watch this. These people are not fooling around."

"I know." I feel my mouth go dry and try to swallow. I do not enjoy pain, but even though Connor's seriousness scares me, I cannot deny that the prospect of being punished by him entices me.

He pulls me to my feet. I barely reach his chin, and I am dwarfed by his size, his power. I want him to embrace me, to swallow me whole, but instead, he grabs the handcuffs and forces my hands above my head, locking them to a chain hanging from the ceiling. I cannot help but wonder how many people have been restrained like this, begging for mercy, fearing for their life. It almost seems disrespectful as I try to inch myself closer to Connor just to feel him.

"Comfortable?" he asks with a smirk.

"No." I have to stand on my toes to relieve some of the strain on my wrists, but the handcuffs still hurt. "But I guess it is not supposed to be."

He nods and removes the belt from my neck. He sets up a video camera on a tripod in front of me. "Can you play the scared, kidnapped girl for me, Brooke?"

Something about the situation and the vulnerability causes my pussy to ache. Connor is calm and collected, but part of me wants to see the beast lurking beneath. It surfaced in his confrontation with Crow, and the brat inside me wants to lure it out, to see it in its passionate, dangerous glory.

I want to be taken by the Beast.

A red light appears at the top of the camera, and Connor steps in front of it. "Mr. West, as you know, we have your daughter. Pay what you owe, and she will be let go." He turns towards me, grabs my hair, and yanks my head back. "If not …" He opens his switchblade and lets the cold steel slide down my cheek. "We *will* hurt her."

I play along for now. I beg for my life, I shake my head and pull the chains holding me. It is not easy; I can feel myself getting wet as the helplessness and restrictive position causes a wildfire in my pussy. Connor steps behind me, leaving me to face the camera as the fake tears stream down my cheeks. Those tears have saved me from many a speeding ticket.

"AAAUGH!"

The belt hits my exposed butt and catches me by surprise. The pain is sharp but does not linger. He is holding back. To my surprise, it only adds to my arousal.

"Please, I beg you … stop!" I cry in front of the camera.

Another hit. It stings, but I do not want it to stop, despite my cries indicating otherwise.

I cry and scream as my body shakes, but it becomes increasingly hard to mask my excitement as desperation and pain. There is an addictive rhythm to the sound of leather against my skin and I start to wonder if I could come from the whipping alone.

"I think that will do," Connor says. "They can edit a nice ransom video from that. You did a …"

"Is that all you've got, Daddy?" I suggestively put my ass out towards him. "I thought I had been *bad.*"

He appears in front of me. His face is set in stone, his jaw clenched. "Are you sure you want to walk down this road, Darling?" There is an ominous tone to his voice that frightens me, but I have received a taste now. I want more.

"I barely felt those hits," I lie, answering his question.

His eyes become narrow slits. "You are being a provocative little brat …" I can hear the leather belt squeak as he clutches it in his hands.

"What are you going to do about it?"

He smiles, but there is no warmth. He rolls up my shirt, exposing my breasts, before stepping behind me again.

"I am going to punish you, Darling. Fifteen lashes. And you are going to count them."

I smile to myself. "I'm not sure that … AAAAAAAH!"

This is different. This is intense. This *hurts.*

"Count it!"

"O… One!" I stutter as the next hit lands on my back. My breath catches in my throat, and I can feel the tears well up in my eyes, but every hit still sends torrents of pure, unfiltered lust soaring through my body. "Two!"

Why the hell am I enjoying this?

"FUCK! Three!" I bite the inside of my arm. It is aching from the strenuous position, and I feel like a slave girl receiving her just punishment. I cannot escape, I cannot prevent it from happening. Would he stop if I asked him to? Somehow, it does not feel like an option. "SHIT, FOUR! Hit me *harder,* Daddy!"

I know it is a mistake. That pushing his buttons is risky, but I cannot help myself. The hits increase in force.

Harder.

Lust and pain collide in a dangerous, addictive cocktail. My voice struggles to call out the numbers. We are up to twelve now.

Harder.

The world seems to melt away as my mind tries to cope with the intensity, the overload of emotions, sensations, and agony. The thirteenth hit makes me scream louder than ever before.

Harder.

Too hard.

CHAPTER SIX

CONNOR

The belt draws red lines across Brooke's untouched back and ass. Seeing her shake with every hit, hearing the lust in her screams, all makes me hard. She teases me, challenges me to hit her harder. I know I should hold back, that I should suppress the part of me that finds some joy in this part of my job; I pride myself on my professionalism, but the sadist in me do enjoy tormenting the captives for the camera.

I pour all my strength into the last few lashes and hear a change in her voice.

"Please, Connor, please stop," she screams, her voice hoarse and barely able to speak through the tears. "It's too much!"

Hearing my name causes me to freeze. Countless men and women have begged me to stop, to release them, but it never affected me before. I throw the belt aside as I feel a lump in my throat.

"Darling, are you alright?" I ask as I walk in front of her. Tears stream down her cheeks, and she's sobbing loudly.

She does not answer right away. The lust is still there, lingering in her eyes, but there is fear as well. "I … I'm okay. It just … it hurt a lot."

I wipe a tear away and stroke her hair. "You did well."

She smiles. "Thank you." As my hand graces her cheek, she closes her eyes and sighs as if she is soaking up the few drops of affection.

"What did we learn, baby Darling?" *God, I want to kiss her so bad.*

"That I shouldn't challenge you, Daddy."

I know her arms must be hurting at this point. Several deep, red grooves from the handcuffs are visible on her slender wrists, but I do not want to take her down just yet. I circle her for a bit, taking in her body, the marks that my belt has left on her. I have marked her, she is mine, and my mind pushes away any thought of what I will do when her father inevitably pays his debt. I do not want to let her go. I kneel and kiss the marks on her back. Her body shivers and the sobbing turns to whimpers, then to quiet, muted moans. Her body is warm despite the low temperature in the room, and my hands gently caress her buttcheeks and thighs as my mouth journeys lover, kissing the long, red lines on her lovely butt.

"Do you like this, Darling?"

"Yes, Daddy. Very much."

My hand moves up her inner thigh, and she spreads her legs for me even though it puts further strain on her aching wrists. I trace the outside of her sex, occasionally journeying inside before pulling out again. I can sense her frustration, but I have no intention of bringing her to orgasm at this point, this is merely a distraction from the pain and discomfort.

She groans as I stand up and unlocks her handcuffs from the chain. "That was cruel," she says and looks at me with a disappointed frown. She winces as the blood rushes back into her arms. I can tell that she wants me to hug her, to show her the affection that she yearns for. Part of me wants the same, but I am resisting it. My mind is torn between the calm professional and the soft lover who wants nothing more than to take her in my arms and run away from it all. As she stands there, naked from the waist down, her breasts still visible beneath the rolled-up tank top, I can feel the beast inside, feeding on my desire. Its growl is distant for now.

I lead her to a stained mattress with an itchy blanket in the corner. She does not protest at the sight of the crude accommodations, though her eyes cannot hide that she is used to far better than this.

"You need to rest, Darling," I say and grab a heavy chain that is connected to the wall. I lock it around her neck with a padlock. "I don't know how long you'll have to stay here." The thought of having Brooke as my captive for days is alluring, and I cannot help but smile as I speak.

I get up to leave when she grabs me by the wrist.

"Stay."

I look down at her. My heart flutters and my cock fills with blood. The complexity of her being is evident in her expressive eyes and in the word that still hangs in the air between us. She is begging me to stay, but she is also telling me to. The confident woman and the vulnerable, frightened girl merge and make me want her more than ever. No man would be able to resist Brooke West at this moment.

She smiles as she notices my hesitation. "Please. Take your clothes off and lie here with me."

The request is absurd, yet I comply. I remove my T-shirt and bare my tattoos to the chilly air of the cell before removing my boots and pants. The cold, calculated voice that usually guides my actions when I am working screams at me, fills my head with curses and reminds me of who I am. I kidnapped Brooke. I took her against her will, and I am tasked with motivating her father to pay by any means necessary. Yet I cannot resist.

I lie down on the old mattress. The worn springs dig into my back, and a faint, moldy stench hangs about it, but it is soon vanquished by the fragile aroma from Brooke's hair as she lays her head on my chest. We do not speak; words seem superfluous, and none comes to mind. I imagine we are somewhere else, far away. Perhaps back in the Caribbean, on the gorgeous beach near my apartment, soaking in the sunlight and pondering whether to take a swim or a nap. The thought is soothing and appealing, but the sound of the chain around Brooke's neck forces me back to reality.

I feel the cold steel on my skin. She is my prisoner. I am her captor. This cannot end well.

A pleased sigh escapes her as her hand gently rubs my chest. The chain connecting her handcuffs clatter with every movement, further solidifying the absurdity of the situation. I pull the dusty blanket over us and feel the warmth of her tiny body against mine.

What are you doing, Connor? I think as I kiss her forehead.

CHAPTER SEVEN

BROOKE

His broad chest rises and falls beneath my cheek, and his strong, slow heartbeat echoes like a drum in my head. My own body refuses to stay calm, however; arousal and lust battle against anxiety and fear on a battlefield with no apparent winners. I ache for him, I want him, and it only gets worse as my fingers trace the elaborate tattoos on his chest. His scent overwhelms me, and I am still wet from his short, but effective, fingering a few moments ago.

He is a criminal, Brooke, the rational voice in my head says, but it is growing fainter with every moment. There is something here, between us. I try to push away any thoughts of the long-term implications and consequences, but I cannot ignore the cold, heavy steel chain locked around my neck, tethering me to the wall and this depressing place. It presses on my throat and reminds me of what Connor is capable of.

The whipping was exhilarating, but he went too far. I know it was my fault, my fault for prodding the beast beneath, and the skin on my back and butt still burns as a reminder.

A reminder that also serves as encouragement.

There is a primal force underneath his cool exterior, and I cannot help but feel that I have only gotten a small taste of the pleasure to be had. I can feel his power as I lay against him, my leg resting on his muscular thigh. He feels rigid as he stares at the ceiling, likely struggling with similar thoughts to mine. My hands move away from his chest, down, over his ripped abs, following the trimmed trail of pubic hair. He twitches but does not speak.

I want him to fuck me. To unleash the beast and take me hard. I have not held myself back when it came to having sex as a teenager and since, but Connor is a man. A real man. It is not just his muscles, his tattoos, those are superficial. It is his power, his smell, all of it. The composure, the deep, commanding voice. I want it all inside me.

I bite my lip to try and contain the mounting desire as my hand finds his tip. The handcuffs make it all feel awkward, yet the touch of his erection fills me with joy. He wants me. Badly.

I have barely touched his mighty cock before Connor jumps to his feet and stares at me with a scowl on his face. "Stop that!" he says.

"But ..."

He shakes his head. "You asked me to lie with you. I did." I try to listen, but his towering erection is distracting. He rubs his forehead. "I think this might be a mistake."

No. I do not accept this.

The time for rational thinking is long passed. I am chained and handcuffed in a dour cell, kept against my will by a man I do not know, yet I refuse to register his words. I want his cock. And I am used to getting my way.

"You think I'm a mistake, Daddy?" I say, fluttering my eyebrows. I spread my legs wide as I stretch my arms over my head. The sound of my chains echoes in the room as I arch my back, pushing my shapely chest forward. "Do you not want me?"

He takes a deep breath. I can see the struggle in his eyes.

I writhe on the mattress as I moan. "Please, Daddy …" I fill my voice with air, licking my lips without ever losing eye contact with my prey. "I want you to fuck me."

"This is not …" he tries, but his cock retains its majestic erection.

I get on all fours and crawl towards him. "I'm all yours, Daddy. Take me." I go as far as the chain allows me; it pushes against my throat as I take the tip of his dick in my mouth. I am having trouble breathing as I pull against my chain collar like a dog fighting its leash. I let my tongue dance across the part of his cock I can reach, showing my affection, my willingness.

He could pull away. He could lock the door and leave me in the darkness.

Instead, he grabs hold of my hair and pushes his cock inside my mouth as deep as he can. I gag on his massive member as I smile. I won. I look up at him and see the calm, rational man is gone. The dark eyes are fire, his jaw clenched. The Beast is awake, even if Connor is still in control.

"You are a naughty little girl, Darling," he says. Power drips from every syllable and makes me wet. He pulls his cock out, leaving a long strand of drool hanging between its tip and my lip.

I smile. "I know, Daddy. Please … punish my pussy. Fuck me, stretch me, make me *yours.*" This is not dirty talk. I mean every word.

"You call that begging, Darling?" He takes hold of the chain and pulls me to my feet, choking me. "You can do better."

I let out a gasp as his fingers slip inside me. Somehow, he finds spots of intense pleasure that I have never discovered on my own. "Please, Daddy! I will do anything! I want your cock so bad!"

"That is better."

He travels deeper inside me as he uses the other hand to pull the chain upward.

"FUCK!" I cry with a shallow voice. "Daddy, come on … please!"

His fingers leave me. I am a desperate mess, trying to grind my pussy against his thigh, but I cannot reach.

"Show me how much you want it, Darling," he whispers, kissing my neck. I swear his lips are electric. "Suck them." He holds his fingers up in front of my face. They glisten in the dim light.

I do not hesitate as I suck my juices from his fingers. I have never tasted myself before, and it feels forbidden, taboo.

Fantastic.

He pushes his body against mine, forcing me up against the wall. The rough, cold concrete sends a shiver down my spine, a stark contrast to the burning heat emanating from his impressive body. He bends his knees slightly, allowing his cock to slip in between my legs, teasingly rubbing against my slit. He is still holding the chain, and the other hand exits my mouth, grabs the handcuffs, and pulls my arms over my head.

"You smell so good, Darling," he whispers as he kisses my neck. The chain around my neck tightens, and the steel links pinch my skin. Every breath is laborious and arousing; it is as if my skin is twice as sensitive as usual, registering every slight twitch of his muscles. I give in to the helplessness, the knowledge that I belong to him. A profound sense of freedom and lust washes over me, and all the tension, anxiety, and fear leaves my body in a liberating moan.

"Daddy, I want you inside me! I'll be a good girl, I'll be your slave, just … just fuck me!"

I can feel his smile against my neck. He presses me harder against the wall, and the touch of his tip against the outside of my pussy is making me soaking wet. He grabs my hair and lays me down on the mattress, on my back, with what can only be described as forceful tenderness. He towers above me, his face covered in shade. He is remarkable, imposing, majestic as he looks down at me, his body poised to attack. I raise my hands above my head, feel the handcuffs around my wrists, my restraints, my prison, showing him that I am his to take. I spread my legs wide, exposing the pussy that is already dripping for him.

He closes in. Slowly. A vision of barely contained lust. I know he wants to ram his hard cock deep inside me. His eyes are swallowing me whole, but he is determined to make me wait. His body is almost horizontal above me, kept up by his straightened, strong arms. His cock teasingly grazes my stomach. The smile is playful and menacing at the same time. I writhe beneath him, pushing my pussy up towards his cock, but he dodges it.

I whimper, frowning at him.

"What are you, little Darling?" He starts massaging my clit. "I want you to tell me what you are to me."

Rays of pleasure shoot out from my clit, and I struggle to focus on his words. "I … I am yours, Daddy." The words are caught between short breaths and moans. "Your slave, your Darling." I pull my wrists apart as far as I can, feeling the steel against my skin. "Fuuuuck …"

"I will take care of you, Darling," he says and uses his hand to guide his cock, rubbing the tip cock against my clit. "I will keep you safe."

The words sizzle in my mind. They are a promise, a contract, and it makes me stupidly horny to hear them spoken in that deep, sexy voice. My body shivers as he teases me, and when he lets a small part of his cock slip inside, barely entering me, I push against it, trying to force him in deeper.

"Don't be hasty, Darling." His burning eyes undress me, remove my skin, and bares my soul. It is the hottest thing I have ever seen. I have never done drugs, but if they are half as addicting as having Connor's eyes on me and his cock in my pussy, I get why people get hooked.

This is torture! Every time his girthy cock takes a peek inside me, it vanishes a moment later. The chain burns my neck, the handcuffs sear my skin, both reminding me that I have no control, and it is both frustrating and liberating.

"Are you ready, Darling?" His breath on my ear warms my entire body.

I nod. "Yes, Daddy. I am ready for you."

My pussy explodes in an intoxicating cacophony of pain and pleasure as his cock fills me. It is a glorious entrance, worthy of fanfare. I have never been stretched like this before, and for a second, I fear that he might be too big. He rests, allowing me to get accustomed to his girth.

"Fuuuck, Daddy!" I open my eyes and stare into his. The connection is immediate and intense as we smile at each other.

"Darling … Brooke." The sound of my name carries immense weight. He starts thrusting into me, gently. I can sense the beast beneath every movement as he struggles to contain it. "You are mine now. This pussy … it belongs to me."

I nod as I bite my lip. "I know. It … it is what I want." I put my arms around his neck, as tight as my restraints allow. "Now … fuck me, Daddy. Harder." I smile, letting him know it is alright. "Unleash the Beast."

He hesitates for a moment before his lips split and his eyes narrow. "As you wish."

My body drowns in a flood of pure lust as his thrusts increase in force. There is still kindness in his eyes, but the beastly part of him has joined the fray and is driving his huge cock deeper inside me than I ever thought possible. Every little part of pussy grinds against the silk-like skin that covers the rock-hard force of nature between his legs.

"Daddy!" My screams fill the room. Some words are unintelligible, simply being an outlet for the massive sexual energy my body cannot contain. "Connor! Daddy!"

He growls as his hips clash against mine. The chain to my collar clatters with every thrust. It is simple and effective; there is no delicacy to his fucking, only brute strength, and it is driving me insane with desire.

"Choke yourself, Darling," he commands.

I unwrap my arms from his neck and grab hold of the chain, pulling it above my head. Not so hard as to cause me any harm, but enough to elevate the beastly thrusts even further. It is dirty, brutal sex like I have never experienced before.

I can feel his strong abs tense as he nears climax. He will get there before me, yet the newfound submissiveness inside me finds it fitting.

"I am going to come inside you, Darling," he groans, staring me in the eye.

I nod. I have not been off the pill since I was a teenager. "Yes, Daddy! Please do!"

"FUUUUUUUUUCK!"

He spills into me as the bear-like roar attacks my ears, underlines his domination. Every muscle in his body threatens to burst through the skin as the massive veins in his neck pulse, and I feel appreciated, worshipped, beautiful to have received his load. It was amazing. It …

It is not over.

He opens his eyes, sweat glistening on his forehead. His demeanor changed in an instant. The Beast is subdued.

Yet he is still fucking me.

"You are amazing," he says with a smile. His cock softens, but not by much, and it still fills me. His movements are meticulous and calculated as he places his hands under my hips and lifts my lower body from the mattress. "You are a goddess, Darling."

The words sound like a choir of angels in my deliriously horny mind. "Connor …" I whimper as my eyes close. I need to shut off at least one of my senses to cope with the incredible sensations bursting from my pussy.

"I'm right here, baby," he says. His pelvis rubs against my clit in a beautiful duet with his cock's magic thrusts.

"Mmmm …" Words no longer materialize in my mind. I only imagine colors, sensations. I cannot focus on anything but the sex. I no longer register the restraints, the cold, the room.

"Can you come for me, Brooke?"

I nod. I let go. I throw myself off the cliffs and into the infinite, orgasmic abyss. He embraces me as the orgasm tears through me, getting more intense every second until I scream. He is still fucking me, but he does it slower. Slower. He carries me down from the mountain, out of the abyss, and he finishes by kissing me gently.

A professional, indeed.

CHAPTER EIGHT

CONNOR

It takes me a few moments to realize where I am when I wake up. I am cold and naked, lying on a stinky mattress next to a gorgeous, chained girl. I have woken up in sadder locations next to far worse, yet my first thought is to curse my weakness and poor judgment. This was supposed to be a quick, easy job. Collect the fat paycheck and return to the quiet life, possibly for good this time, and now I have gone and fucked it up. And fucked the target.

Just get up and leave. Lock the door, come get her when the job is done. The cold, unsympathetic voice in my head no longer sounds like my own and makes me sick to my stomach. My body refuses to obey its commands; few people have managed to sneak past the fortified defenses I have built after a life of harsh truths and cruelty, but watching Brooke sleep is causing the walls to crack.

The hair, messy after the intense, life-altering sex last night, crowns her innocent-looking face. The small nose twitches as she dreams, and despite the uncomfortable steel holding her wrists and neck, she looks peaceful as she lies there in a fetal position. My heart swells as I stare at her flawless beauty, and I know that I could never get up and leave.

My God, she looks amazing. My hand gently follows the curve of her naked butt without waking her, and I start getting hard. She deliberately woke the primal part of my being last night, the part that has often gotten me into trouble and fights, the part that I fear, but the result was not harmful. It was amazing, intense sex. I let go of my doubts and fear, and she somehow managed to tame the Beast. I smile at the memory of being inside her as I stroke my cock.

An idea forms in my head, and I cannot help but smile. She brought the animal forward, and it is insatiable. Insatiable and playful.

I grab a padlock from the table nearby and carefully lift her hands over her head without waking her. I lock the handcuffs to her collar chain.

"Mmhmmm …" she groans. Still asleep, she adjusts her body to lie on her back, and the movement causes her legs to open up, exposing her carefully trimmed pussy. It calls my name, and I am not one to refuse such an invite when it is presented like this.

"Mmm … what?" Her drowsy voice is mumbled as she wakes to the feeling of my fingers caressing her pussy. "What the fuck?" Brooke panics for a moment and pulls violently at her chains. "What are you …" Her voice is harsh at first, but she pauses when our eyes meet. It is as if it takes her a few seconds to realize where she is and what is happening, but the wide-eyed, frantic expression on her face is soon replaced by a crooked smile.

"Good morning, Darling," I say as my finger moves teasingly up and down the outside of her vagina. "Did you sleep well?"

She moves on the mattress, trying to get comfortable despite the chains. "Like a baby. Mmm … don't stop …" Her legs open wider, and I have to resist the urge to lie on top of her. The whimpering, muted moans make me hard.

"You don't get to decide if I stop or continue, Darling," I say with a smile.

She nods and bites her lower lip. "I know, Daddy."

"If you want me to continue, you have to answer a few questions."

She raises an eyebrow and looks at me, but any protests she might have are overridden by an airy gasp as my fingers enter her.

"Who was the first guy you fucked, Darling?"

The hazel eyes stare at me. "What?"

I stop my exploration of her pussy.

She groans. "Fine! Jeremy Johansson, the first year of high school."

I continue, hitting a spot that makes her arch her back with delight. "Very good. Who was the first man to make you come, Darling?"

She hesitates for a second and pulls her chains in frustration when I stop again. "Man? It … it was you, Daddy."

"Don't lie to me, Darling." I pinch the edge of her pussy, causing her to wince in pain.

"I … I'm not, I swear!" Her voice is pleading; she is telling the truth. "The others … it was good, some of it, but they never … succeeded." There is no pain in her eyes as she meets my gaze, only affection. "They never focused on me."

I try to suppress a smile. The revelation fuels the fire in my chest as I push my fingers deeper inside her.

"Fuck, Daddy! That is so good!" She sucks her lips in between her teeth as her eyes close. Her abs tighten and her chest heaves, pushing her lovely round breasts towards the ceiling.

"Have you ever been with another woman, Darling?" I already know the answer. It was evident in her hesitation at my last question. I slow down my elaborate exploration of her pussy to encourage a quick answer.

She nods, her eyes still closed. "Y… Yes," she moans. "My roommate, Jennifer. We … we were drunk."

"Did you enjoy it?"

"I did, Daddy." Her body wriggles closer to me in an attempt to lure my fingers deeper inside, and it causes the chain around her neck to tighten.

"Do you like being choked, Darling?" I lean in and start licking her clit.

"FUCK!" She coughs as the outburst is restricted by the chain. "Yes, Daddy, I love being choked."

The sight of the harsh, thick steel against her slender neck makes me even harder, and I start rubbing my erection lightly against the mattress to satisfy myself. My fingers are soaked by her juices, and I am tempted to enter her now.

I stop licking her for a moment. "How many men have you fucked, Darling? Be honest."

"Please, Daddy, don't stop!" She stares at me with the eyes of a submissive, a woman desperate for my touch. The lust has taken hold of her body, and all she wants is the satisfaction that only I can give her. It is exhilarating to behold. "I … I'm not sure!" Every muscle in her body tightens in frustration. "Twelve! It's twelve!"

I reward her. My thumb rubs her clit while my finger massages the spots inside that I know will drive her crazy.

"What do you want me to do to you, Darling?"

"Anything … you … want … Daddy." Her voice is frail and distant. "I belong … to you. I'm your Darling, your slave. Fuck me … whip me … chain me in a cage. I don't care. I … I just want your cock." Her eyes are half-open as she wrestles herself away from the infinite chasm of pure desire for a short moment. "And I want you." Her voice is calm, serious. Committed. "All of you."

I am ready to come just from hearing her words. They grab hold of my heart and my cock, and it takes everything I have to not fuck her right away. Instead, I keep her tethering on the edge, walking the line. She slips back into the pool of pleasure, only surfacing from time to time to scream in frustration.

She is mine. She belongs to me, as does her pleasure, her orgasms. At this moment, I feel like I could conquer the world.

CHAPTER NINE

BROOKE

My body is no longer my own. It is not because of the chain around my neck or the handcuffs digging into my skin. It is not because I am a captive, chained to a wall, unable to escape. It is his hands, his tongue; every slight movement, every lick keeping me suspended in an infinite, maddening moment of blissful torture. I am elated and frustrated, joyful and angry. I never want it to end, yet I want nothing more than to climax and find release for the lust that is threatening to split my body in half. Every moan and twitch is by his will, and I would never want it any other way.

I am his willing victim.

How does he do this? My thoughts are blurry as seconds feel like hours. I have no idea for how long he has kept me walking the tightrope at this point. He is no longer interrogating me, but I would not be able to answer anyway. The only word that manages to escape my drooling, whimpering mouth is "Please …"

Over and over again.

"Please …"

Suddenly, his fingers leave me. His tongue no longer explores my body.

"No … NO!" I pull at the chain like a madwoman, screaming in frustration. "You … can't … NO!"

Then I feel it. The tip. The magical, teasing tip.

"Yes! Please, Daddy!" He could offer to release me at this moment, offer to give me everything I ever wished for in life, and I would turn it all down to feel his cock inside me. "Fuck me, Daddy!"

He enters me. It is gentle, warm, affectionate, nothing like the beastly pummeling he assaulted me with last night. My pussy embraces him as every nerve ending inside explodes. He lifts one of my legs with his strong arm, opening me further, allowing him to hit spots of undiluted ecstasy that I never knew existed.

"You are perfect, my Darling."

It feels like his dark, deep voice causes his pelvis to vibrate against my clit.

"My slave."

The word echoes in my entire body.

"My Brooke."

I cannot hold back anymore. Every thrust of his massive cock is like a small orgasm, full of passion, lust, and love. It feels like I have crossed a threshold in more ways than one. I want to embrace him, to hold him, but my restraints prevent it. I pull at them so hard that it hurts, but the pain only fuels the fire inside me.

"I … I am going to … come, Daddy!" I whimper and wheeze, barely able to form a sentence. "Can I … Can I come, Daddy? Will you come with me?"

Our bodies melt together as our eyes meet and he nods. Such power and purpose in one single movement of his chiseled chin. Heat radiates from his body into mine as his thrusts become more fierce, driving us both over the edge as our grunts and moans join in an angelic choir. He is harder than ever before, filling me, threatening to tear me open with his might. One arm supports my leg, the other's hand is on my butt, digging its nails into me.

I come. The sight of Connor becomes hazy as the intense, unbelievable orgasm tears through my body. It feels like my skin is on fire as his cum fills my pussy. His cock twitches inside me, but there is no roar this time, no beast. Instead, there is a smiling, sweating man that looks at me with more love than I ever thought I would experience in my entire lifetime. My body still shakes and his cock still fills me as he leans in and kisses me.

"You are amazing," he says.

"You're not too bad yourself."

We laugh. I have not heard him laugh before, and the deep chuckle fills the depressing room with joy. He pulls out; I can feel his cum trickle down my pussy, and without him inside me, I suddenly become aware of the pain in my wrists. And the hunger.

"I'm really hungry," I say and try to sit up.

"We can't have that." He unlocks my cuffs from the chain before getting up. He puts on his jeans and smiles at me. "I'll be right back."

As I watch him leave, I try to focus on the ripples of pleasure that still grip my body, but I suddenly feel alone and scared. Connor's presence has managed to keep the thoughts of my predicament at bay, but it all comes crashing back as I sit alone in my cell and stare at the bruises on my wrists.

He returns a few minutes later with a humble bowl of oatmeal. "This is not a five-star establishment, I'm afraid," he says apologetically as he hands me the bowl.

"It's alright." I try to operate the spoon while holding the bowl, but the chain connecting my cuffs is too short. "Please?" I nod at the handcuffs.

"Of course."

Connor removes the handcuffs and even unlocks the chain from my neck. The lack of restraints makes me feel oddly light, but also more naked than I already am. It is the first time I am unrestrained in his company since the abduction, and the shift in the dynamic is evident to us both.

"If …" The question burns my tongue, but I fear the answer. "If I try to run now, would you stop me?"

He sits down next to me and scratches his forehead. "Yes."

My stomach feels cold, but it warms a moment later at the sight of his smile.

"But only because I cannot imagine being without you, Brooke."

He places his arm around me, and I immediately feel safe again. Comfortable. I rest my head on his shoulder.

"I … I'm not sure I would survive if I allowed you to escape, in more ways than one." His voice darkens, and the reality of our situation starts to sink in.

I do not know if it is the intensity of the entire ordeal, the mindblowing sex, or if there is truly something deeper at play, but I feel the same way. I snuggle in closer to him to let him know. I can feel his stubble on my forehead, the warmth of his naked upper body against my bare skin.

"How is this even going to work?" I ask, cursing my rational self for taking control of my voice instead of enjoying the tenderness.

He shrugs. "I don't know. We'll *make* it work. Your father will pay soon, then we figure it all out. I have money. Lots of it. It tends to solve a lot of problems."

"It also tends to cause them."

"True. But we …"

The song 'Bad Boys' by Inner Circle suddenly fills the room. I can feel Connor's phone vibrate against my thigh.

"That could be the call telling us that you're free to go," he says. He kisses me on the forehead and stands up. He puts the phone to his ear and winks at me. "It's Connor."

I take another spoonful of oatmeal. My mind struggles to comprehend what comes next. Would I go with him? Away, out of the country? I would have to give up my studies, my friends … it all seems unreal. I look up at Connor and I am overwhelmed by his raw confidence, his magnetism. Yes. I would go anywhere to be with him. Everything will be alright as long as we are together. Everything will be …

"He did *what?*" His face darkens. "That is not going to happen," he says and clenches his jaw. He hangs up and slams the phone onto the table.

"What is wrong?"

Connor's nostrils flare like a raging bull, and it seems like he is struggling to tame his rage. "Your father …"

"Yes?"

"He called the cops. This just got a lot more complicated." He looks at me with a mix of anger and pain. "Crow is on his way. He says we need to step this up. Torture you."

I feel like the oatmeal is ready to come back up. "Connor …"

"I'm not going to let that happen, Brooke." He tries to sound determined and certain, but he cannot hide the doubt. "But we do have to step it up."

"How?"

He sighs. "We will have to involve the Boss."

TO BE CONTINUED

ABOUT THE AUTHOR

J.D. Ackles is a career-minded woman who pours her dark fantasies of bondage and captivity onto the page in her spare time. She has published countless short erotic stories under her other pen name Jessica Ackles, all focused on BDSM in some form.

Apart from the dirty writings, she is an avid reader, a casual gamer, and a collector of handcuffs and other steel restraints – jewelry comes in many shapes and sizes. She can occasionally be found updating her Instagram profile (@jessicashackled) with kinky pictures and new releases.